BRONTO EATS MEAT

Story and pictures by
Peterodactyl Maloney & Felicia Zekauskasaurus

DIAL BOOKS FOR YOUNG READERS NEW YORK

E
MAL

To Michael Maloney, whose hospital stay inspired this tale

Published by Dial Books for Young Readers
A division of Penguin Putnam Inc.
345 Hudson Street
New York, New York 10014
Copyright © 2003 by Peter Maloney & Felicia Zekauskas
All rights reserved
Designed by Kimi Weart
Text set in Franklin Gothic
Manufactured in China on acid-free paper

1 3 5 7 9 10 8 6 4 2

Library of Congress Cataloging-in-Publication Data
Maloney, Peter, date.
Bronto eats meat / story and pictures by Peter Maloney and Felicia Zekauskas.
p. cm.
Summary: A young plant-eating dinosaur, having accidentally swallowed a boy,
has three choices for getting rid of his stomachache.
ISBN 0-8037-2791-7
[1. Apatosaurus—Fiction. 2. Dinosaurs—Fiction. 3. Sick—Fiction.]
I. Zekauskas, Felicia. II. Title.
PZ7.M29735 Br 2003
[E]—dc21   2002001451

The artwork in this book was created with pencils,
pastels, and gouache.

Bronto was your typical young brontosaurus.

He could eat a whole tree in a single bite . . .

and he often did.

One day, Bronto came home with a *terrrrible* stomachache.

"It must be
something you ate,"
said his mother.

"But I've eaten
nothing but bushes
and flowers and trees,"
said Bronto.

When the pain got worse, Bronto's parents rushed him to the hospital in a special dinosaur ambulance.

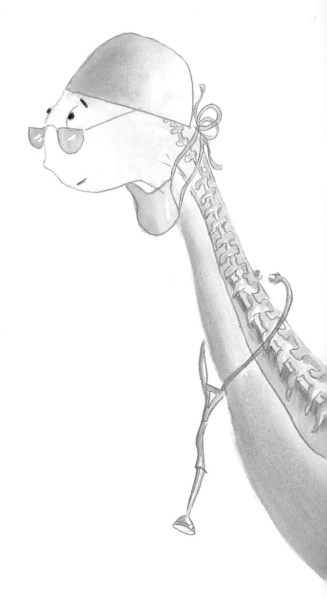

The doctor who examined Bronto was so pale,
you could see right through his skin.
"He must be a Paleontologist," whispered his mother.

"Since you can see through my skin, I'd like to look through yours," said the doctor. He took an X ray of Bronto. It showed his ribs, his stomach, and . . .

a little boy named Billy!

Earlier that day, Billy had been hiding from
his pesky sister . . .

GULP!
—down he fell until he landed with a SQUISH! in a bed of leafy green slime.

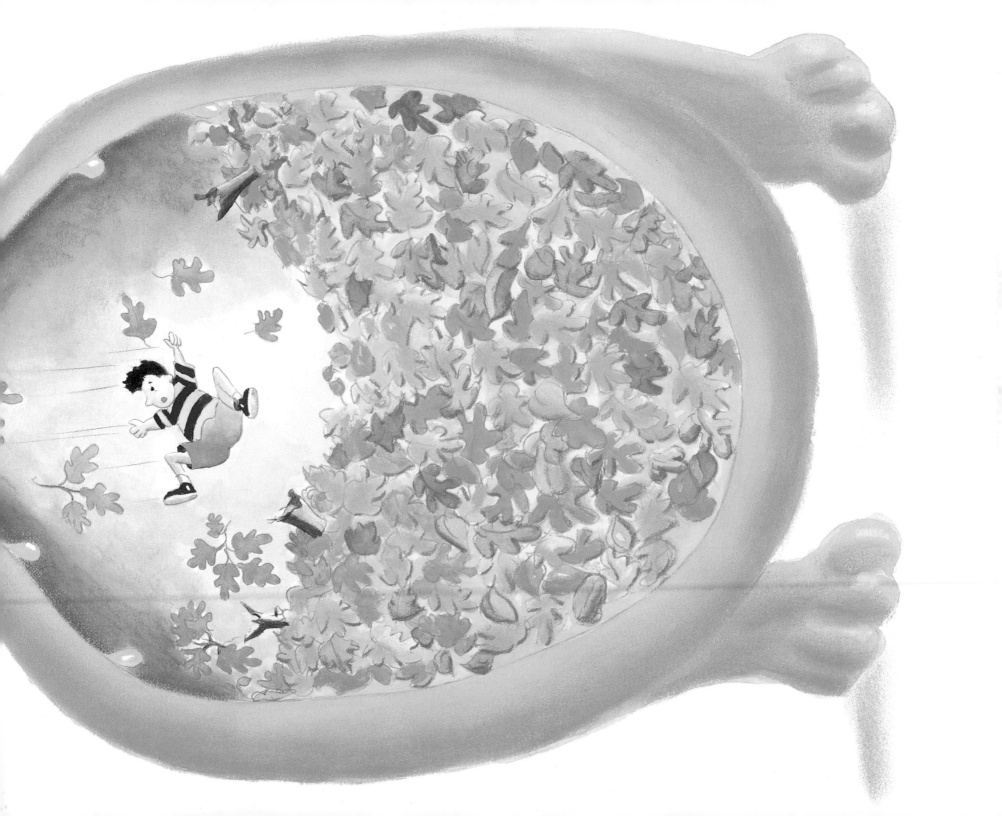

Now, Bronto was a leaf eater, or an *herbivore*. He didn't like to eat meat like his carnivorous cousin, T. Rex.

"That boy in your belly is the problem," said the doctor. "We must get him out—and there are three ways to do it.

"Number one is vomiting—disgusting,
but effective.

"Number two is . . . well, we all know
what number two is.

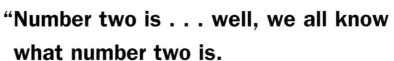

"And number three is gaseous expulsion,
by which I mean burping, or—um . . . *you*
know what I mean."

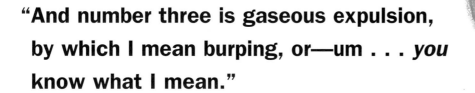

Bronto and his mother discussed what to do.

So the doctor asked the
nurses to bring one hundred
cans of Slurp 'n' Burp soda.

Soon Bronto's stomach began to gurgle and rumble.

B-U-U-U-U-U-R-R-

Billy shot through the air like a human cannonball . . .

R-R-R-P-P-P...

and landed with a THUD! in his own backyard.

"And where have you been, young man?" asked his mother.

"I was eaten by a brontosaurus!" said Billy.

"Sure," said his mom, "and I've just been appointed governor of New Jersey! Now go wash up before your father sees you."

Though it was completely true, no one ever believed Billy's story.

"Brontosaurus?" said his sister. "That's preposterasaurus!"

As for Bronto, he now watches what he eats . . .

at least most of the time.

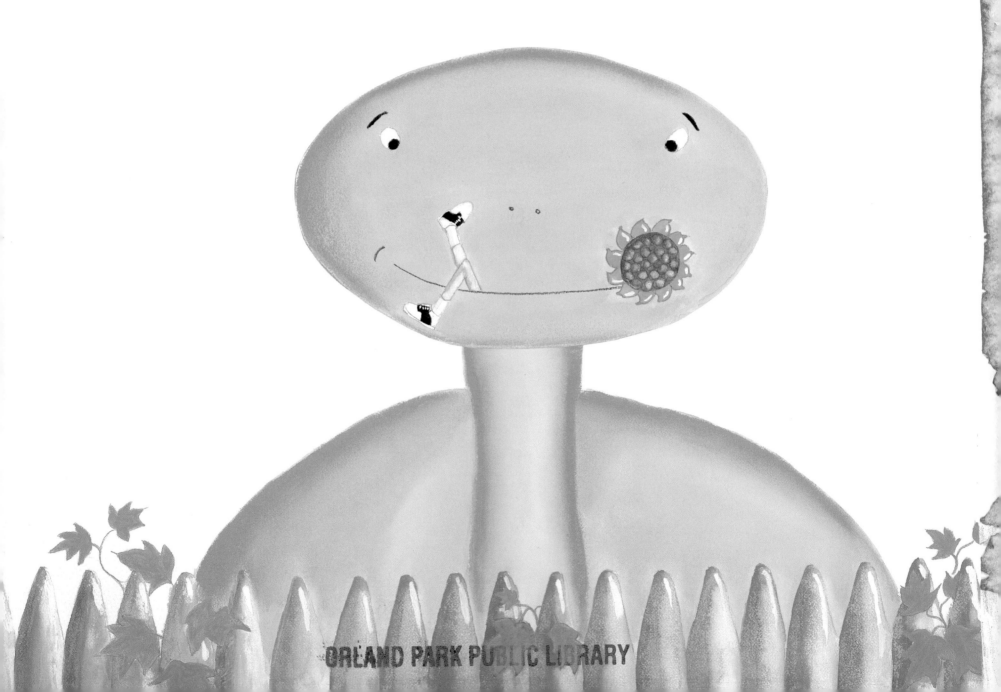